Eckhart Tolle
Robert S. Friedman
Milton's Secret

An Adventure of Discovery through Then, When, and the Power of Now

Illustrated by **Frank Riccio**

 Namaste Publishing

 HAMPTON ROADS PUBLISHING COMPANY, INC.

Cover design by Bookwrights Design
Cover art by Frank Riccio

Hampton Roads Publishing Company, Inc.
1125 Stoney Ridge Road
Charlottesville, VA 22902

434-296-2772
fax: 434-296-5096
e-mail: hrpc@hrpub.com
www.hrpub.com

Co-published with

Namaste Publishing

Vancouver, Canada
www.namastepublishing.com
General inquiries: 250-954-1693

If you are unable to order this book from your local
bookseller, you may order directly from the publisher.
Call 1-800-766-8009, toll-free.

Library of Congress Cataloging-in-Publication Data applied for.

ISBN 978-1-57174-577-4

10 9 8 7 6 5 4 3 2 1

Printed on acid-free paper in China

To my children,
Jonathan, Matthew, Marc, and Sophia,
who give me inspiration every day.
—Robert S. Friedman

for my godchildren, Justin, Francesca, and Jackie boy
—Frank Riccio

Milton, a bright and cheerful
boy, loved life. He loved his mom
and dad and his nice house.
He loved his cat Snuggles.

He loved school and his teacher, Mrs. Ferguson.

He loved to play dodgeball at recess.

But most of all, he loved going to the ice-cream shop with his dad after dinner to get his favorite sundae.

One day at school, he was playing catch
with his friend, Timmy, when a mean-looking,
much bigger boy named Carter walked over to
him, screwed up his face, and said, "Milton.
What kinda name is Milton? You weirdo."

Suddenly, he pushed Milton so hard that he
stumbled and fell to the ground, scraping both
knees.

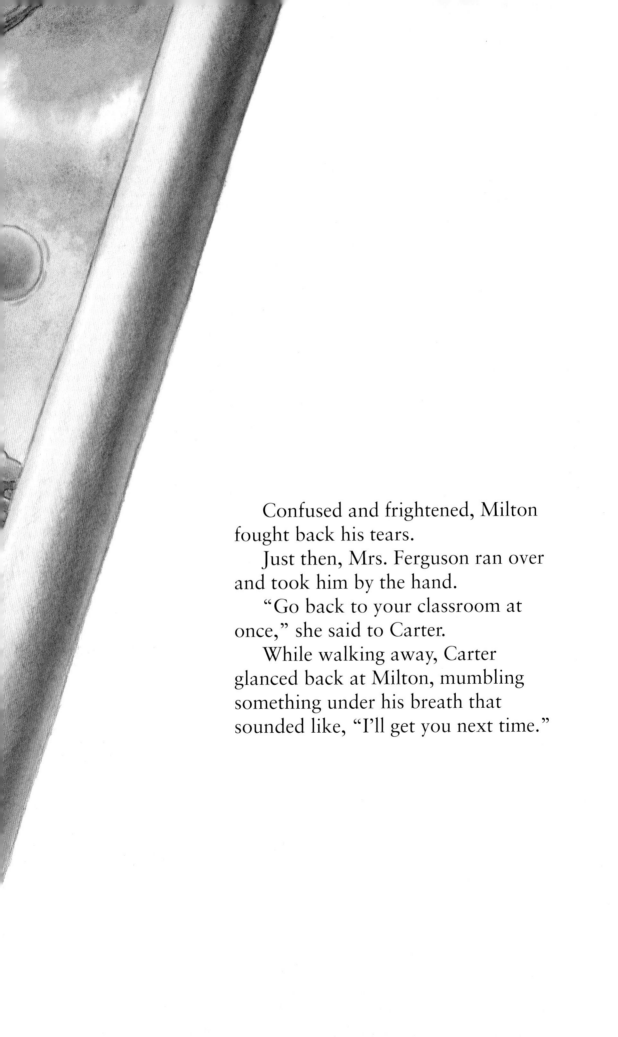

Confused and frightened, Milton fought back his tears.

Just then, Mrs. Ferguson ran over and took him by the hand.

"Go back to your classroom at once," she said to Carter.

While walking away, Carter glanced back at Milton, mumbling something under his breath that sounded like, "I'll get you next time."

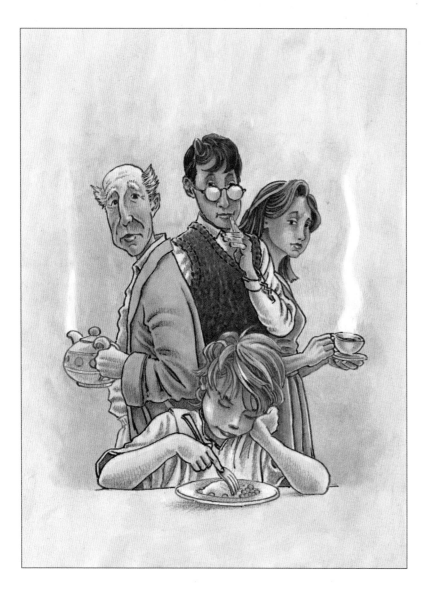

In the evening, his parents and his Grandpa Howard, who was visiting with them, noticed he wasn't the same Milton. He didn't smile much, he picked at his food, and he wasn't even excited about going to the ice-cream shop after dinner.

"What's the matter with you, Milton? Is something wrong?" his mother asked.

"No, nothing," said Milton.

That night, Milton couldn't get to sleep. He was thinking about what happened—and what *would* happen when he ran into Carter next time.

"Why did he pick on *me,*" he kept thinking, over and over.

"Why *me!*"

"What's he going to do to me *next time?*"

The more he thought about all of this, the more frightened he became. He thought about it so much that he became more and more scared until he completely forgot that he was in a warm bed in his little room.

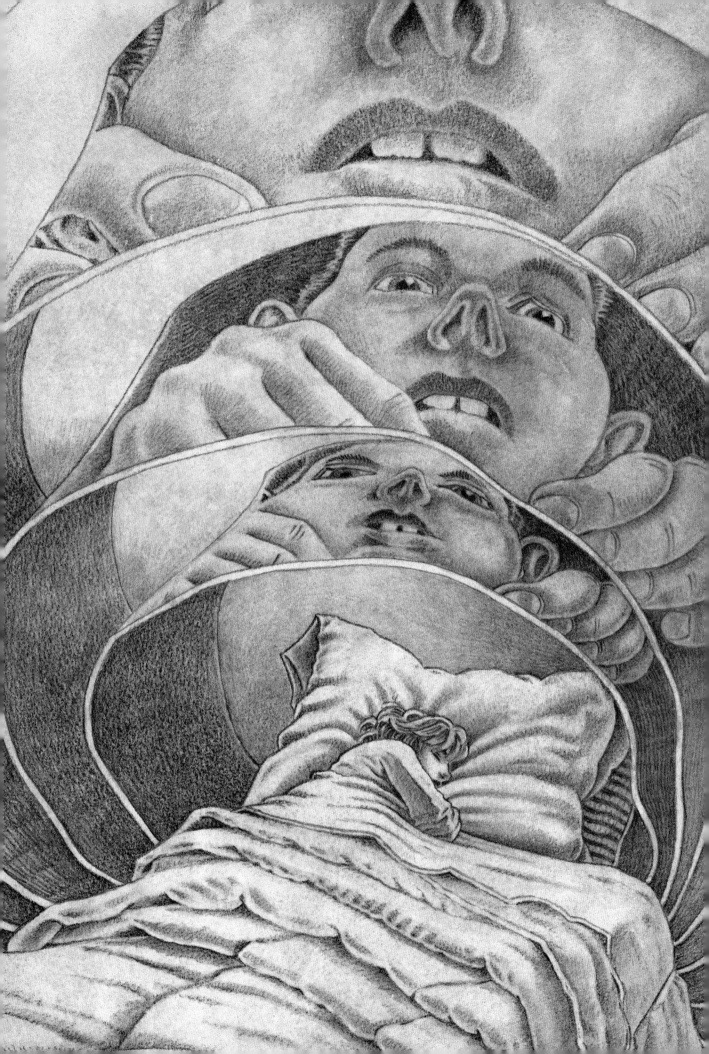

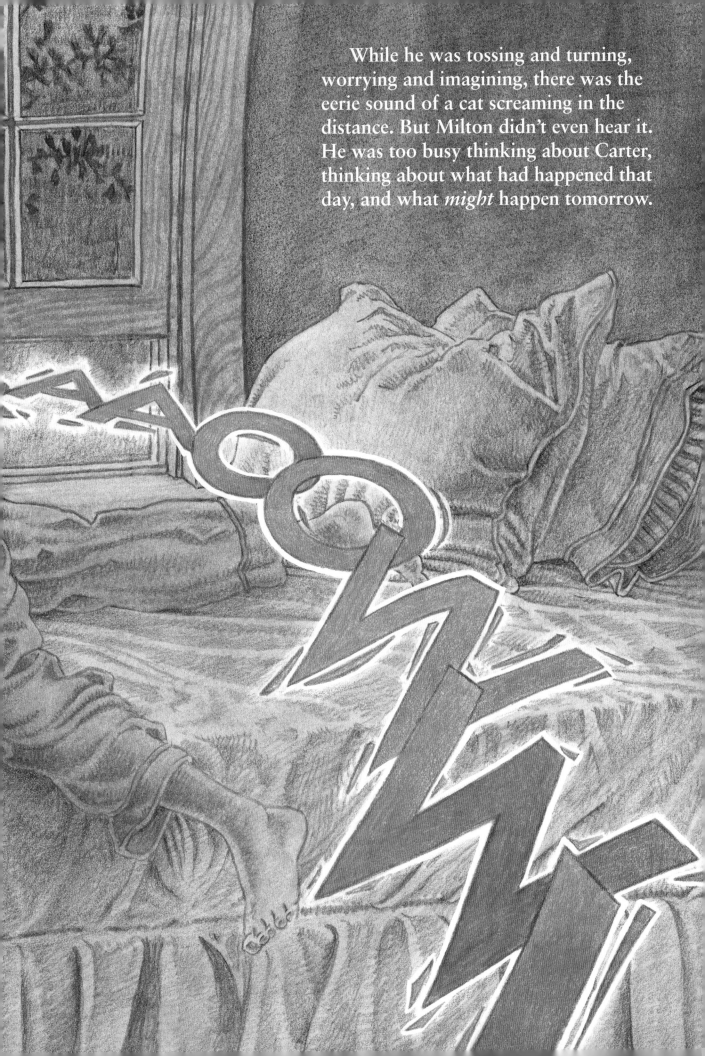

While he was tossing and turning, worrying and imagining, there was the eerie sound of a cat screaming in the distance. But Milton didn't even hear it. He was too busy thinking about Carter, thinking about what had happened that day, and what *might* happen tomorrow.

In the morning, Milton was so tired he couldn't stop rubbing his eyes.

He headed downstairs to do what he did first thing every morning—give Snuggles his breakfast. But when he opened the door to the kitchen, oh what a sight! There was Snuggles all beaten up. His right paw was bleeding, it looked like a chunk had been taken out of his left ear, and he was missing several patches of hair.

Milton let out a scream. "Oh, poor Snuggles! What happened to you?"

He picked him up straight away and rubbed his cheeks against his furry body.

"I bet it was that Brutus. He's supposed to always be locked in his yard. Poor Snuggles."

His parents and his grandpa, hearing Milton scream, came running to see what was going on.

"Look what happened to Snuggles!" Milton blurted out. "It must have been Brutus."

"Who's Brutus?" asked Grandpa Howard.

"He's the Doberman across the street," Milton replied. "His owners haven't trained him right, and he's a mean dog."

Milton took Snuggles to the sink in the kitchen where he and his mom washed Snuggles's wounds and bandaged his ear and paw.

Once Snuggles was all cleaned up, Milton carried him to the couch in the living room to cuddle and comfort him.

Grandpa Howard sat in an armchair watching Milton.

In no time at all, Snuggles, resting on Milton's chest, was purring blissfully. The purring was so strong that it made Milton feel warm and tingly inside, all through his chest and back.

This set Milton to wondering.

"Grandpa," Milton asked, "How can Snuggles be so happy just after being beaten up?"

"Milton, cats are not like humans. Snuggles
can easily let go of what happened yesterday, and
he doesn't worry about tomorrow. He lives in the
Now. That's why he's happy even though not long
ago Brutus was attacking him. Most people don't
live in the Now because they think of yesterday or
tomorrow most of the time. And a lot of the time
they are unhappy."

Milton paused for a moment then asked, "The
Now? What does that mean, Grandpa? What's
the Now?"

"Milton?"

"Yes, Grandpa."

"Pay attention to what's around you. Look . . .
listen."

Then, spreading his arms as wide as he
could, Grandpa said, "*This* is the Now."
"Oh, wow!" exclaimed Milton.
"Wherever you are," said Grandpa, "that's
the Now. You just have to pay attention."

"Grandpa," Milton asked, "Can *you* always live in the Now like Snuggles?"

"Sometimes I can," said Grandpa Howard, "But, no, not always."

Just then, Milton's mom called from the kitchen. "Come and get your breakfast, Milton, or you'll be late for school."

That day at school, he
watched out for Carter. He
looked for him down the halls,

in the lunchroom,
in the bathroom,
on the playground.

He didn't want to run into
him again.

In the evening after dinner, Milton and Grandpa were in the backyard. Milton looked worried again, so Grandpa said to him, "Your mom and dad think something has been bothering you, Milton, and I noticed it, too. Do you want to tell me about it?"

Milton could feel the fear inside him start up again.

After a while he said, "A boy in the sixth grade pushed me down in the school yard—and just because my name is Milton. He's so big, Grandpa, what if he tries to do it again?"

Grandpa, holding up his right hand, signaled with his index finger. "If he ever tries to hurt you again, promise me you'll tell your mom or dad at once, and you should also tell your teacher."

"Okay, I promise," said Milton.

"When did this happen?" asked Grandpa.

"Yesterday."

"I see," said Grandpa, "yesterday. That was When it happened. But it's not happening now, is it?"

Milton, angry and frustrated, said, "Of course it's not happening now. But I'm worried he'll try to do it again."

Grandpa replied, "If he does, it will be Then, won't it? You're worrying about Then and thinking about When. Aren't you forgetting something? Then and When are in your head. They are not here *Now,* are they?"

"I don't understand," said Milton. "Then and When are in my head? What are you talking about?"

But Grandpa didn't respond. He just looked at him with deep understanding, and smiled.

That night in bed Milton started to worry again, thinking about Carter and what he did and what he will do next time.

Thinking. Thinking. Thinking.

When he finally fell asleep, he found himself in a strange dream.

He is running down a dark street as fast as he can. His heart is beating in his throat. He is running away from someone who is getting closer and closer. It's Carter.

Then suddenly, at the end of the block there is a growling, fierce-looking dog. It's Brutus. If he stops running, Carter will get him. If he keeps going, Brutus will do to him what he did to Snuggles.

His legs are wobbly and about to give way. Milton stops dead in his tracks.

What can he *do?*

Just then, he looks to his right and sees a little door. It looks like the entrance to some kind of store.

He quickly opens the door and, to his surprise, finds himself inside the ice-cream shop!

"Ah, here you are. I've been waiting for you, Milton," the ice-cream lady says.

"I'm being chased by a boy named Carter, and there is a big dog who wants to hurt me, too," Milton blurts out.

"Nobody's chasing you, and there's no dog out there going to hurt you. It's all in your head."

"No, it isn't," says Milton. "They're out there waiting for me."

"Sit down, honey. Let me show you something," says the ice-cream lady.

"The new sundae-of-the-month . . . choco-cadabra?"

"No, it's something even better," she replies.

She reaches under the counter and takes out a ball of glowing white light on an ice-cream dish. Milton has a strange feeling that the light is alive.

"That's no ice cream," says Milton. "What is it?"

"It's a light bubble, honey. Isn't it beautiful?"

Right then, the light bubble goes "POP" and bursts into a shower of sparkles. Milton is left staring at the empty dish.

"Oh no, it's gone," says Milton.

"No it isn't," says the ice-cream lady. "The light just doesn't like to be looked at, so now it's hiding. See if you can find it."

Milton looks all around the room. But no matter how hard he looks, he can't see any light bubble. Suddenly, he notices a strange noise like a little electric engine.

Purrr—purrr. Purrr—purrr. . . .

That sounds like . . . Snuggles, of course! There he is, sitting on the counter with his eyes half closed, purring blissfully. What's he doing in the ice-cream shop anyway?

For a moment, Milton thinks he sees a glow coming from inside Snuggles, and he asks the ice-cream lady, "Is the light bubble hiding in Snuggles?"

"Well done," she says. "But the light is not a bubble anymore. It's just light. And the cat is purring because he can feel it, and it feels good.

"Where else is the light hiding?" she then asks, as she smells the flower on the counter.

Milton sees a tiny glow in and around the flower.

"Is it . . . ?" he starts.

"Yes, it is," the ice-cream lady interrupts. "The light is in the flower, too. That's why it's so beautiful. Anywhere else?"

Milton looks into her big, brown eyes.

"Your eyes are so bright," he says. "I think the light is in you, too."

"You're right, honey. You see, the light is in everything, always. It gives life to everything."

Milton looks down at this body. "What about me? I can't see any light inside me."

"No, you can't see it in yourself, but you can always feel it."

"I can?" asks Milton.

"Sure, it's easy. Let me ask you a question: Are you alive?"

"Of course, I'm alive," says Milton.

"Are you just saying that, or can you actually feel that you are alive?"

"What do you mean?" asks Milton.

"Start with your hands. Can you feel the light inside them?"

Milton closes his eyes for a moment. "I'm getting a tingly feeling inside my hands."

"That's it," says the ice-cream lady. "You're feeling the light. Can you feel it in your feet, too?"

"Yes, I can."

"Your arms and legs?"

"Yes."

"Can you feel the light inside your whole body?"

"My whole body feels kind of warm and tingly."

Milton looks around the room. "Everything looks a bit different, too. Just like when my grandpa was talking to me about the Now."

"That's right, Milton. Grandpa showed you the outside of the Now. And this shows you the inside."

"The inside of the Now?" asks Milton.

"Yes, when you feel the light inside your body, you are in the Now. And you're not scared anymore. The light helps you feel strong."

"Really?" says Milton. "That's great."

"And now that you know what it's like, you can feel the light inside you whenever you want to."

"Oh, that's double great!" exclaims Milton.

"Let's keep the inside of the Now a secret just between the two of us, okay? Most people are not ready to understand this."

"No problem," Milton replies.

"No problem. No problem," Milton was still murmuring to himself when he woke up from his dream and found himself in his warm bed.

He opened his eyes.

The half-moon was casting its pale light on his bed. The tree in the yard outside his window was very still. Only a few leaves moved in the breeze. There was the noise of a car passing by . . . then it was still again.

Even now he could feel the tingling inside his whole body.

For no reason at all, Milton felt happy.

But on the school bus that morning, Milton started thinking and worrying again, and he felt scared of going to school.

Then he remembered what the ice-cream lady had told him in the dream. "Feel the light inside your body, and you won't be scared anymore."

Milton decided he had nothing to lose by trying it out. So he did. There was that tingling again in his hands, and then in his feet . . . then he could feel the light inside his whole body again.

Now I am in the Now, thought Milton. *It feels good to be in the Now.*

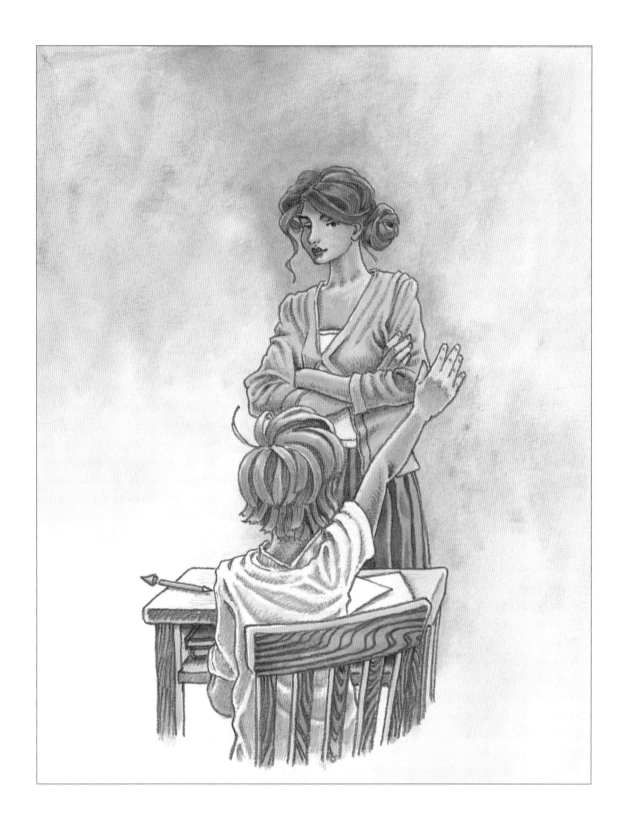

That afternoon in class, Milton raised his
hand and asked to go to the bathroom.
Mrs. Ferguson smiled and nodded her head.

Milton was washing his hands in the bathroom and enjoying the feel of the cool water when the cubicle door behind him opened, and someone stepped out. Milton glanced in the mirror and saw the figure of a big boy looming behind him. The boy looked at himself in the mirror for a moment, paying no attention to Milton.

How unhappy he looks, thought Milton. Then suddenly, oh no! He realized the boy was Carter.

Carter gave the short hair on his head a rub with both hands, put on his cocky face, and walked out of the bathroom.

He's unhappy, so he wants to make others unhappy, too, thought Milton. But I'm not going to be scared of him anymore. Milton felt the light in his body. I'm not going to be scared of anything or anybody anymore.

That afternoon Milton got home just in time to say goodbye to Grandpa, who was getting ready for the drive back home.

"Grandpa," Milton said excitedly, "I'm not scared anymore—of Carter or of anybody. And I know the secret of staying in the Now, just like Snuggles."

"What is it," asked Grandpa?

Milton got close to Grandpa and whispered in his ear, "You have to find the *inside* of the Now."

"The *inside* of the Now? Where do I find that?"

"I can't tell you. It's a secret. But I know you can find it out for yourself."

Namaste Publishing

publisher of Eckhart Tolle's *The Power of Now,*
A New Earth, and other healing and transformational
books, audios, and DVDs
www.namastepublishing.com • 250-954-1693

HAMPTON ROADS
PUBLISHING COMPANY, INC.

publishes books on a variety of subjects,
including spirituality, health,
and other related topics
www.hrpub.com • 434-296-2772